# Deep Fate

A New Mineral is Discovered

William H. D. Coleman

Sunshine Horizon Publishing

I am very grateful to people I admire. Who have inspired and helped me with writing. These people all know who they are, and many others, who don't know they helped me but inspired me.  Some have left the Earth to be in the stars, and under the sea.

I love my family and friends so much.

Thank you.

"Look and you will find it.
What is unsought will go undetected."

# Contents

# I

# The Depths

A bove and below the Pacific Ocean an ambitious scientific endeavour is taking place. One team is on the sea bed of The Mariana Trench. The other, support team, is on the sea surface. Guided by their advanced over-the-horizon computer systems, both teams embark on a ground breaking mission. The target is one of the most unexplored places on Earth.

The weather's unusually calm. The nearest tropical storm is over two hundred kilometres away. The air hangs humid on the surface ship, making droplets form on the metal deck. In contrast, it was nicely air-conditioned on the undersea sub, with humidity kept at 40% and the temperature at a constant twenty-three degrees Celsius.

The Mariana Trench is the deepest part of the world's oceans. At a depth of approximately 36,070 feet (nearly 11,000 metres), it is known as Challenger Deep. Located in the western Pacific Ocean, this trench is where the Pacific Plate is forced under the Mariana Plate, reshaping the Earth's crust. The pressure here exceeds 1,086 bars, with temperatures near freezing. At sea level, the atmospheric pressure is about 1 bar. This means that the pressure at the bottom of the trench is over 1,000 times greater than at sea level.

The advanced computer system, affectionately called GEORGE (Geological Exploration and Resource Geolocation Engine) is helping a team of ten, with its precise calculations and predictive models. Ten above the sea, and five below the sea. The team includes engineers, geologists, mineralogists, and scientists all aboard the advanced research vessel, the *Deep Explorer Surface Ship (DESS)*. They monitor progress as the drilling team, far below, drill deeper and deeper into the Earth's crust. Deeper than ever before. Buzzing sounds of electronic beeps, and the smooth calming sound of whirring air conditioning units.

The massive cathedral-sized drills of the *Deep Explorer Drilling Station (DEDS)* penetrate the seabed with unrelenting force. The screeching and grinding sounds of the drills sound like London underground trains, roaring through the tunnels, carving their way underground. Rocks being crushed and crunched like ice cubes, being demolished by your teeth, after getting inside your mouth while drinking cola, in your favourite pub garden in the summer.

The undersea drilling station is an old repurposed oil rig. It had its large stabilising legs removed and was then submerged. It's been placed directly on the sea bed. The platform's been repurposed for drilling while under the sea, partly to aid with cooling of the massive drill bits, and partly due to the depth and logistics of retrieving samples, to and from the support vessel.

The drilling team of five, get to and from the undersea drilling station by submersible, housed and maintained in the

*Deep Explorer Surface Ship.* The submersible is called the *Deep Explorer Sub (DES).* This is manually operated. Included with the DES is a fast remotely operated vehicle, which is a submersible one-twentieth the size of DES, that can go to and from the surface ship within twenty minutes, delivering samples and returning supplies to the DES.

The drill tip is now at an unprecedented depth of forty-nine kilometres. The team monitors the operation from the control room of the surface ship. Lights flicker, instrumentation buzzes. Every sediment layer and rock formation is analysed in real time. GEORGE, designed to adapt and respond to geological anomalies, suddenly signals an alert. The alert chimes in a rhythmic tone. There's an unusual formation fifty kilometres below the sea bed, precisely where the computer system predicted the mineral would be. The drilling team retrieves the core mineral sample and sends it in the remotely operated submersible to the *Deep Explorer Surface Ship.*

Encased within the extracted cylindrical section of rock is what appears at first glance to be a simple mineral. As the geologists and mineralogists examine it, they realise GEORGE was correct. The system knew exactly what the mineral was, and where it would be found. It is unlike anything previously seen, ever. The mineral exhibits unique properties that suggest its formation under extreme pressure and unique geological conditions, was nothing short of a miracle.

The drilling team comes across an unexpected anomaly within the same core sample. It's a piece of rock. Granite in appearance, with glistening quartz. Granite forms from silica-rich magmas, thought to form by heat or water vapour at the lower crust, rather than by decompression of mantle rock, as is the case with basaltic magmas seen deep within Earth. This granite rock is not any ordinary rock. The simple granite-like rock contains a microchip. A fossilised microchip. The microchip's encased in a layer of granite rock that preliminary tests suggest is 500 million years old. The presence of such an advanced technology embedded within ancient geological strata sends shockwaves through the team.

How could a seemingly modern and sophisticated device be fossilised within such ancient material, fifty kilometres below the Earth's crust?

GEORGE recalibrates its systems for further analysis, and the team sets up for extensive testing of the predicted mineral and unexpected rock containing a fossilised microchip.

# 2

# The Silurian Connection

G EORGE knew, with a probability of over 95%, that the team would find this new mineral. Find it at this precise location, fifty kilometres below the Earth's crust. There was 0% indication, from the computer system, that a fossilised microchip would be found, let alone inside a rock, at the same location.

The control room aboard the *Deep Explorer Surface Ship* purred with nervous energy. Scientists, engineers, and technicians surrounded the glass-enclosed examination table where the fossilised microchip lay. It lay there like a precious artefact in the British Museum. The room was a mosaic of diverse accents and languages, a testament to the global effort behind the mission. Whispers and nods among the eager team. But at this moment, all voices converged on one burning question.

How could this technology exist in rock, millions and millions of years old?

Dr Elise DuPont, a leading palaeontologist and engineer, stood at the forefront of the discussion. She tapped on the holographic display, bringing up geological timelines, fossil records, and a series of images comparing the microchip's intricate patterns to naturally occurring crystalline structures.

"We need to tread carefully," Elise began, her tone firm but measured. "Very carefully. This could very well be a bizarre natural phenomenon. There are crystalline formations in nature that mimic structured patterns. We can't jump to conclusions. Keep Occam's Razor in mind. You all know Occam's Razor's principle, which suggests the simplest explanation is usually the correct one. Keep in mind, it's highly likely this is all a hoax,... a joke."

"But crystalline formations don't generate data signals," blurted Dr. Torsten Berg, a physicist who specialised in energy systems. "GEORGE detected extremely faint electromagnetic remnants when we extracted this sample. That's not natural"

The room fell silent as Elise magnified an image of the fossilised microchip's surface. The engravings delicate, yet precise, glimmered under the laboratory lights.

"Applying Occam's Razor, it's highly probable we are indeed looking at modern-day technology which is a hoax. Or, if not a hoax, it has somehow, inexplicably entered one of the underwater volcanic shafts along the Mariana Trench,... how you ask? Think back to the year 2004. Tectonic plate movements throughout the Pacific Ring of Fire, after the Indian Ocean Tsunami,... which would have thus buried objects at these immense depths. The Ring of Fire contains over 750 and 915 active or dormant volcanoes, and 90% of the world's earthquakes". Members of the team slowly nodded in agreement. "However, on the opposite end of the scale. If this is something else and it's as old as tests indicate" she said, "we're looking at evidence of advanced technology that predates not just human civilisation but even the dinosaurs."

A few of the team sniggered, while the others stood in wonder, eyes wide and mouths opening in slow motion.

"Which brings us to the Silurian hypothesis," Torsten said, leaning forward. He swiped through his tablet, projecting an academic paper onto the central screen. "I'm sure you lovely people have heard of it, no? Quick revision for everyone,... Schmidt and Frank posed the question years ago. *If an industrial civilisation existed millions of years ago, would we even be able to detect it in the geological record?*"

The hypothesis ignited an animated debate. One faction of the team leaned toward scepticism, citing the improbability of an advanced civilisation arising so far back in Earth's history, eliciting Occam's Razor. Another faction, led by Torsten, argued that the microchip could be a missing piece in humanity's understanding of deep-time evolution and technological progress.

Elise attempted to mediate. "Let's examine this logically. If a civilisation existed millions of years ago, what evidence would survive? Fossilised bones? Ruins? Most structures would have eroded or been destroyed by tectonic activity over such vast timescales."

"Exactly!" Torsten burst out. "That's why we haven't found any traditional markers of such a civilisation. But this microch ip,... this fossilised microchip, if it's real, could be the evidence. What we need is absolute dating of this rock."

The team agreed, and preparations began for isotope analysis by GEORGE to confirm the age of both the fossilised microchip and the rock. Meanwhile, discussions turned somewhat speculative.

If the microchip was genuine, who or what created it?

Could Earth have hosted an advanced civilisation long before recorded history?

As they waited for the isotope analysis test results, the team huddled to explore the wider ramifications of their find.

Torsten summarised everything he knew. "If this microchip is authentic, it forces us to reconsider not just Earth's history but humanity's place in it. It aligns with the concept of cycles, with civilisations rising and falling over aeons, leaving behind traces only detectable by chance."

Elise added, "It's extremely unlikely, but, and I mean but,... If intelligent life has risen and fallen on Earth before, it raises questions about our own trajectory. Are we destined to follow the same path?"

No one said it out loud, but they were thinking about the ethical dimensions of their discovery.

What would happen if the world knew?

Could such knowledge destabilise societies, religions, or global economies?

By the end of that day, preliminary GEORGE isotope analysis revealed a truly jaw-dropping result. The rock, encasing the microchip, was over 500 million years old. This placed its origin firmly in the Paleozoic era. The fossil was created within plus or minus one hundred thousand years of that date. There were traces of Amino acids in the rock packed full of nitrogen and carbon-rich compounds. These include 20 amino acids that life on Earth uses to build proteins and all four of the ring-shaped molecules that make up DNA, including adenine, cytosine, guanine, and thymine. The room fell into stunned silence as the weight of the evidence sank in.

Elise broke the quiet. "If this is what it appears to be, we've just uncovered something that rewrites history,... possibly the future too. We need more than one anomaly to confirm this hypothesis. We need to keep drilling. We need to find more evidence."

As the team on board the *Deep Explorer Surface Ship* prepared to resume drilling, they couldn't shake the profound implications of their find.

Had Earth hosted advanced civilisations long before humanity's rise?

Was the Silurian hypothesis more than a thought experiment?

The answers lay in the uncharted depths of the Mariana Trench and the mysteries yet to come.

The drilling team got into the submersible and started their descent. The *Deep Explorer Sub (DES)* creaked and hissed with precision, as it aimed for the underwater rig, eleven kilometres below. The HEPA-filtered air, nice and cool with a steady breeze from the onboard air conditioning, helped to cool down the crew's excitement. After transitioning eleven kilometres the team uncoupled and made their way gingerly onto the *Deep Explorer Drilling Station (DEDS)*.

# 3

# Voyager

The fossilised remains of the microchip rested in a sterile containment chamber. It bristled with promise and wonder. Its surface is magnified and displayed across the room on holographic screens. Every line, curve, and indentation was meticulously scanned and analysed. The initial mystery of its existence had deepened. There were small engravings on its surface that were unlike anything seen before, yet oddly familiar. Barely visible to the naked, but clearly seen on the magnified screen.

The weather system was closing in. Fairly close at twenty-five kilometres, the effects of the tropical depression were being felt by the crew. The ship had a state-of-the-art automatic stabilising buoyancy system, so the vast majority of the crew had no sea sickness. That didn't stop a few of the crew, needing time out to go and look at the horizon.

Dr. Elise DuPont stood before the team. A new holographic projection floated behind her like a ghost from the past, watching over her. On one side was a detailed image of the fossilised microchip's surface, clearly showing what appeared to be microchip component markings. On the other side was an image that looked strikingly similar in simplicity to the message sent on the Voyager spacecraft. These were very small engravings, illuminated in sharp relief. The Golden Record, as it was known, was launched into space in 1977 as humanity's message to potential extraterrestrial civilisations. At least half of the image on the fossilised microchip was missing, destroyed by the immense and unforgiving drilling equipment.

"These patterns," Elise began, gesturing toward the fossilised microchip's markings, "share striking similarities with the engravings on the Voyager golden record disc. Look, here" She pointed with her thin and unusually long ring finger.

The comparison was undeniable. Both bore intricate, concentric designs that seemed more symbolic than functional. Elise highlighted key parallels. Spirals, radial lines, and what appeared to be coded sequences.

"What if this microchip is their version of our Golden Record?" Torsten Berg speculated, his voice tinged with wonder. "A message left behind intentionally?"

"But who is 'they'?" someone from the back of the room asked. A slight mocking tone.

Elise didn't answer immediately. Instead, she zoomed in on one of the fossilised microchip's engravings. A dense series of symbols that seemed almost hieroglyphic in nature. "Whoever *they* were," she said finally, "they had a purpose. And I think they wanted us to find this."

The team worked relentlessly, feeding the microchip's scanned patterns into GEORGE for analysis. Its optical recognition systems ingesting everything it sees. Seconds turned into hours before the breakthrough came.

Torsten burst into the control room, his face alight with excitement, yet mixed with fear.

"It's in the DNA," he announced breathlessly. "It's in our DNA. Our junk DNA!".

The room fell silent as he explained.

Using the microchip's engravings as a cypher, the part that looked like the Golden Record, the computer system had identified matching sequences within human "junk" DNA. The vast stretches of genetic material that, until now, were thought to have no functional purpose. The concept of junk DNA was first proposed by Susumu Ohno in 1972. He used the term to describe portions of the DNA in a genome that are noncoding, meaning they do not code for proteins or have any known biological function. All along, there was something hidden in plain sight in junk DNA.

"This can't be a coincidence," Torsten continued, projecting the results onto the central screen. The sequences in the junk DNA mirrored the patterns on the microchip. "It's as if someone encoded a message directly into our own genetic code."

The implications were staggering, awe-inspiring, and complicated. Humanity had long believed junk DNA to be an evolutionary emptiness of nothing, leftover fragments with no discernible role. But now, it seemed that these sequences were anything but random and empty. They were carefully constructed codes that needed decoding.

GEORGE, guided by the microchip's engravings, began decrypting the message in the junk DNA. The process was slow, requiring immense computational power. So much power, all drilling at the sea bed had to stop, while the computer system consumed all available energy onboard.

The initial results were enough to shake the team to its foundations.

The first decoded fragments revealed what could only be described as a repository of knowledge. A repository of knowledge stored within the junk DNA. Stored using similar methods and technology to a blockchain. A dense and structured archive encoded within every human being. Every human being that ever lived, and is alive today, and in the future. The data includes diagrams, mathematical equations, and complex instructions that hint at advanced technologies.

GEORGE concluded that the compressed and encrypted knowledge stored inside the junk part of DNA contained more data and information than everything ever created by modern-day humans. This, combined with all known printed books, digitally created material, every piece of data on the internet, and all languages. Absolutely everything. If current modern-day combined data and knowledge were 10%, the amount of stored knowledge in the junk DNA was 100% of our known knowledge. Ten times as much knowledge as modern-day humans have. Everything to ever know, or be discovered.

"This isn't just a message," Elise said, her voice trembling. "It's a legacy. They didn't just want to leave a record of who they were, they wanted us to understand them. To know where we came from. Everything. But why?"

The revelation sparked a torrent of questions.

If this data had been embedded in human junk DNA, who had placed it there? Why? How?

The timeline stretched back impossibly far, beyond human history, beyond recorded time. 500 million years. Was it possible that humanity itself was the product of this ancient civilisation?

As the team, with the aid of the GEORGE, pieced together the fragments of the initial decrypted message, a picture began to emerge. The ancient civilisation, whoever they were, had faced extinction. Knowing their fate was inevitable, they had encoded the sum of their knowledge and history into DNA, sending it into the future. Figuratively speaking, a message in a bottle. A DNA bottle.

The room was thick with a mix of awe and apprehension. The fossilised microchip had opened a door to a story far older than anyone could have imagined. It wasn't just humanity's history that was being rewritten, it was the history of Earth itself.

Elise turned to Torsten, her voice barely above a whisper. "Do you think they knew we'd find it?"

Torsten nodded. "They didn't just know. They planned for it. This wasn't just survival, it was communication across the ages. How, I have no idea."

The team, overwhelmed by the magnitude of their discovery, prepares to present their findings to the world. But, even as they celebrate, a gnawing question remains.

What other secrets might the microchip, and the DNA, still hold?

Little did the team know, their conversations and video feeds were all being monitored. A specialised team from the Five Eyes (FVEY) intelligence alliance were well aware of what was being discussed. They were about to intervene directly with Elise, to ensure nothing was discussed outside of the mission team. A representative from the FVEY made preparations to communicate with the team on *Deep Explorer* as a matter of extreme importance.

# 4

# The Ancients

The *Deep Explorer Laboratory Rig (DELR)*, is another re-purposed deepwater oil rig. This rig however sits fifty metres above the surface of the sea, twenty-five kilometres away from the drilling location and surface ship.

It looms on the horizon like a beast waiting for its next meal. A steady firm platform in the ocean, teaming with the most advanced technology available to mankind.

The team of three permanently stationed on it can call the rig "Mother". The surface ship comes back to Mother, with the submersible, when required for resupply, maintenance and tests in the laboratory.

The crew are choppered on and off by helicopter when required. The helicopters go to the airfield where private jets whisk the team and visitors away for meetings when needed.

Rumour has it that the Central Intelligence Agency (CIA) funded the rig ten years ago through In-Q-Tel, a not-for-profit venture capital firm based in Arlington, Virginia. Investing in companies to keep the CIA, and other intelligence agencies, equipped with the latest technology.

Regular tropical rain downpours and claps of thunder kept the crew alert to their Pacific location. The frequent lightning bolts, streaking across the sky, with retina-burning intensity, reminded the crew of their vulnerability here in the ocean.

The control room was filled with tension and anticipation as the computer system completed its latest decryption sequence. Elise DuPont and Torsten Berg stood shoulder to shoulder, their eyes fixed on the holographic display. Line by line, the story of an ancient civilisation began to unfold, a tale buried not only in rock but encoded within the very fabric of human DNA.

GEORGE shifted through the vast ocean of data and knowledge. Its instructions were to summarise the who, what, where, when, why, and how. This was succinctly presented to the team. A few years ago, this would have been near impossible. Today with GEORGE and other advanced AI systems, the conundrum of too much data and not enough action is no longer applied. GEORGE and other systems were built for this type of task.

The decoded data revealed the existence of an advanced civilisation that flourished over 500 million years ago, during the Paleozoic Era. The beings from the ancient civilisation were remarkably human in appearance and physiology. They had developed technologies and societal systems that rivalled or even surpassed those of modern humanity. They were humans, just as we are.

This ancient civilisation had harnessed the raw forces of nature, transforming them into clean, sustainable energy. They had achieved breakthroughs in genetic engineering, space travel, and quantum mechanics, achievements hinted at in the encoded knowledge. Cities sprawled across continents that no longer existed in the present day, their architecture harmonising with the natural world rather than dominating it.

"They were us," Torsten murmured, his voice reverent. "At least, a version of us. The way they lived, it's like looking in a mirror."

Their technological prowess extended to the stars. Decrypted evidence suggested that they had established colonies on the Moon, Mars, and Venus. They had even launched exploratory missions beyond the solar system.

But the decryption also revealed a sobering truth. The ancient civilisation's downfall had been both inevitable and devastating. Two catastrophic events coincided, bringing an abrupt end to their golden age. This was why, and the reason they had to encode the sum of their knowledge in the junk DNA. It was the only way the memory and knowledge would survive over 500 Million years.

The first catastrophic event was a biosphere and climate crisis of their own making. Or, as also speculated, the Earth changes naturally with volcanic eruptions spewing massive quantities of gases into the atmosphere. Despite their advancements, their population growth and energy consumption had tipped the planet's delicate balance, alongside massive volcanic eruptions. The computer system reconstructed data showing rising temperatures, acidifying oceans, and widespread ecological collapse. Their ability to mitigate these effects had been outpaced by the speed of the biosphere destruction. They were responsible for destroying their planet, Earth.

The second event was far more sudden for them. An asteroid strike of unprecedented magnitude. The data and knowledge encoded into the junk DNA included simulations of the impact. An inferno that obliterated much of the planet's surface and plunged Earth into a prolonged darkness. This was a life-ending event, but not a planet-destroying event. It left no chance that life would recover, for millions and millions of years.

"They didn't just lose their cities or their technology," Elise said, her voice heavy. "They lost their entire biosphere. The Earth they knew was gone."

Faced with extinction, the ancient civilisation made a desperate choice. They gathered their brightest minds and directed all their remaining resources toward survival. Not on Earth, but beyond it. The decoded messages revealed plans for a mass exodus. A mass exodus to other celestial bodies within the solar system, and beyond.

The Moon and Mars became their primary refuges. Venus served as a short-lived outpost. However, these locations were merely stopgaps. Knowing that their survival required leaving the solar system, the civilisation built several starships. These were self-sustaining vessels designed to carry them to the stars and beyond.

Their destination was Proxima Centauri b. A terrestrial planet in the habitable zone of the Alpha Centauri system. The closest to our Solar System is four light-years or about twenty-five trillion miles away from Earth. Alpha Centauri, the triple star system, became their home. Their refuge, for the exodus.

But even as they fled, they ensured that Earth would not forget them. The microchip, the encoded DNA, and other yet undiscovered artefacts were part of a grand plan to preserve their story. They believed that one day, life on Earth would rise again, and when it did, it would inherit not just the planet but the wisdom of those who came before.

"What does this mean for us?" one of the junior researchers asked, breaking the silence. "If they were so advanced, and they couldn't stop it."

Elise turned to face the team, her expression grave. "It means we need to learn from them. They left us their story for a reason.

They wanted us to know their mistakes, so we don't make them again. They also wanted us to know their solutions. So we could learn from them. They wanted to give us knowledge. They wanted to help us, save us."

The team delved deeper and deeper into the message's remaining fragments. GEORGE further scanned all the data and knowledge, summarising and prioritising what needed to be known, based on the output required by the team. But when you don't know what questions to ask, not knowing what you don't know, where do you start? This is where GEORGE came in.

In a fraction of a second, GEORGE created a list of the top one hundred questions that the team would need to know. With this in mind, GEORGE delved into all the knowledge and extracted the answers within ten minutes to the one hundred questions. The team hoped to uncover more about the civilisation's exodus and the technologies that could shape humanity's own future. The legacy of the ancients was not just a history lesson, it was a warning. A guide. A challenge to avoid the same fate.

# 5

# Material Simulation

ONE YEAR BEFORE THE FIND

I n Singapore Dr. Torsten Berg stood before a room packed with scientists, engineers, and research personnel. There were also Government personnel and agents among the delegates, quiet, discrete, and unassuming. You'd never know.

On the central holographic screen, data streams from GEORGE's latest analyses filled the air. Before drilling for the mineral, which the computer system had a probability of 95% of finding, the system created an exact simulation of the mineral. The team could see and manipulate the mineral, using virtual reality headsets, before the mineral was actually found.

Outside was humid, sticky, and uncomfortable. Low, light grey clouds. Inside the room, it was cool and air-conditioned. Just the right temperature, on the skin. Not too hot, not too cool, about twenty-three degrees Celsius.

"This material, this mineral" Torsten began, his voice barely containing his excitement, "is, sorry will be, nothing short of extraordinary. We need to plan now, how we, and the world will respond.

He explained "Minerals are naturally occurring elements or compounds. Most are inorganic solids, but this doesn't include liquid mercury and a few other organic minerals. They're defined by their chemical composition and crystal structure."

He further highlighted the mineral's most intriguing characteristics. Energy Conductivity. Self-Regulating Heat. Quantum Disruption.

Torsten continued. "The first thing is Energy Conductivity. According to the simulation, the mineral should be able to absorb, store, and release energy at efficiency levels far beyond any known substance. It demonstrates the potential to act as a limitless energy source, capable of powering cities, vehicles, and even spacecraft." There were murmurs among the delegates in the room.

The murmurs died down to a reflective silence. "Second, Self-Regulating Heat. Unlike nuclear materials, it should emit no harmful radiation and require no elaborate cooling systems. Its internal molecular structure will self-regulate heat output, preventing instability." More murmurs, this time louder.

"Third, ladies and gentlemen, please, settle down," Torsten brought the room to a manageable silence. "Quantum Disruption. The most startling property, however, its ability to affect quantum fields in a manner that enables energy extraction from seemingly empty space. This "quantum disruption" mechanism suggests an entirely new way of harnessing energy, one that bypasses traditional fuel-based methods." The murmurs returned, even louder than previously.

"This isn't just a new mineral or element that the system has discovered," Torsten continued. He had to shout above the noise. "It's a new paradigm! A way to generate clean, unlimited energy without pollution, without waste. Without the dangers, we've accepted as the price of progress." The room came back to an audible silence. Stunned silence. You could hear air conditioning fans and elevator doors creaking.

The implications of the mineral's virtual discovery sparked a debate among the assembled experts. Dr. Elise DuPont took the floor, projecting a timeline of human energy advancements, from the discovery of fire, through the Industrial Revolution's reliance on coal, to the transformative impact of oil in the twentieth century.

"Think about what oil did to the world," she said. "It powered industry, reshaped economies and fueled global conflicts. It became the cornerstone of modern civilisation, for better or worse. This mineral has the potential to do all of that and more, but without the destructive side effects."

The comparison was compelling. Oil, despite its transformative power, had also been a double-edged sword, driving climate change and resource-based wars. The mineral, by contrast, seemed to offer humanity a chance to break free from its reliance on finite and polluting energy sources.

However, not everyone in the room shared Elise's optimism.

Dr. Martin Knight, an environmental economist, raised a cautionary note. "The very qualities that make this mineral revolutionary also make it dangerous, If it becomes the foundation of our energy economy, who controls it? How do we ensure equitable access? And how do we prevent its misuse?" Hushed whispers among the audience.

Elise nodded. "Those are valid concerns. But the potential here is too great to ignore. If we manage this responsibly, it could redefine how we live on this planet, and perhaps, even beyond it."

The room grew silent as the implications sank in. The mineral was both a promise and a warning. A reminder of humanity's capacity for innovation and previous civilizations' vulnerability to laxidasical hubris.

# 6

# Quantum Disruption

T he tropical storm had passed with only minor interruptions. There was no damage to the rig or other equipment. One crew member had a twisted ankle, that was it. They'd slipped over in the downpour of rain and misjudged a step in the stairwell.

The dark grey clouds give way to blue skies and sunlight formations, called Crepuscular Rays. Like a personalised laser light show. People call these light patterns the "Fingers of God", "Buddha's Rays", and even "Jacob's Ladder".

The mineral core sample, safely encased in a reinforced glass chamber, is located at the heart of the *Deep Explorer Rig Laboratory*. It shimmers faintly under the intense scrutiny of the lab's floodlight. Its surface radiates a spectrum of colours that seems to shift as if alive. It was unlike anything the team had ever encountered. A substance that defied the properties of other known elements and minerals, except a few of the rare earths such as Promethium, Gadolinium, or Holmium.

The repurposed oil rig lab is a hive of activity as the team conducts experiments on the newly discovered mineral. It's only been two weeks, yet it feels like two years. Two years of excitement and wonder.

The mineral, now dubbed Quantum-42, was proving to be a scientific marvel. Its properties, particularly its ability to interact with quantum fields, held the potential to redefine energy systems, technology, and the future of humanity itself. Just as the simulation one year ago in Singapore predicted.

Dr. Torsten Berg stood before a room packed with eager faces. On the central holographic display, a real-time simulation of the mineral's energy output lit up the room.

"Ladies and gentlemen," Torsten began, his voice brimming with excitement, "what you are about to see is not just a breakthrough, it's a revolution." He coughed in nervous excitement.

The simulation demonstrated Quantum-42's ability to extract energy from quantum fluctuations in space-time. This phenomenon, nicknamed quantum disruption, allowed the mineral to draw limitless energy from what had previously been considered a vacuum. Some people liken this to dark matter. Unlike nuclear power, Quantum-42's energy generation was entirely clean, producing no radiation, no waste, and no byproducts.

The material appeared to be similar to the rare-earth ceramic-like substance. Called rare-earth barium copper oxide (REBCO). If you touch it with your fingers it won't move. But give it a push and it will spin, and spin and spin, without wanting to stop. A superconductor that has near-zero electrical resistance.

Torsten explained the mechanism in simple terms. "Imagine a perpetual energy source that doesn't burn fuel, doesn't require sunlight or wind, and doesn't depend on finite resources. Doesn't pollute, doesn't leave any vapour, not even water, and has no harmful effects like nuclear energy fuel. Quantium-42 taps into the very fabric of the universe, converting quantum fluctuations into usable energy. We don't know how, or what the mechanism is yet. It's almost a miracle."

The room erupted in applause as the demonstration concluded.

Quantium-42 had powered an electrical generator capable of powering both the massive drilling units deep below the ocean and the computer system GEORGE. Between them, they consumed half the electrical power to light up the UK's second-largest city, Birmingham.

The implications were staggering.

A future without fossil fuels, without power shortages, and without the negative environmental impacts of traditional energy sources.

More wondrous was the tiny size of the Quantium-42 required for this power. It was a cube no larger than simple dice, of 5mm (3/16″) but much much lighter, with near zero mass.

The excitement around Quantium-42's energy capabilities quickly turned to its potential applications in advanced technologies. In particular space exploration.

Dr. Elise DuPont had been running simulations on propulsion systems. She took the stage next.

"Quantium-42 isn't just a new energy source, it's the key to space travel. Interstellar space travel," Elise declared. She displayed a series of animations showing how Quantium-42 could power spacecraft capable of reaching distant planets and star systems. Quantium-42 has extremely unusual mass and weight properties. For what should weigh one ton or one thousand kilograms, Quantium-42 only weighs one gram here on Earth. That means it is one million times lighter than it should theoretically be.

How can that be?

Using its quantum disruption properties, Quantium-42-based propulsion systems could bypass the limitations of chemical rockets. By creating localised distortions in space-time, these Quantium-42 fuelled engines could generate near-instantaneous acceleration without expending any traditional fuel.

"This isn't just about speed," Elise continued. "Quantium-42 allows for sustained, long-term energy supply on deep-space missions. Being one million times lighter in weight the possibilities are endless for exciting the gravitational pull of Earth. Colonisation of the Moon, Mars, and even Alpha Centauri becomes feasible. Not in centuries, but in decades."

The room was silent.

The weight of her words sank in. Quantium-42 wasn't just a resource. It was the bridge to humanity's next evolutionary leap. Just like fire, language, the wheel, and mathematics all were before.

As the team brainstormed potential uses for Quantium-42, the possibilities seemed endless.

But the team was also acutely aware of the challenges.

Dr. Martin Knight, the environmental economist, voiced a pressing concern. "If Quantium-42 becomes the cornerstone of our energy economy, how do we ensure it doesn't become another tool for geopolitical control? Who gets to decide how it's used?"

The questions hung in the air, a sobering reminder that even the most promising discoveries carried the potential for misuse.

Later, in the evening, standing at the observation deck of the rig, Elise looked out over the vast, dark ocean. The moon reflecting on the ocean waves. "We're standing on the edge of something incredible," she said quietly to Torsten, who had joined her. "But the question isn't just what we can do with Quantium-42. It's whether we're ready for it."

The mineral's properties raised questions about its role in the ancient civilisation's history. GEORGE sifted through the knowledge repository, stored in the DNA, and confirmed what the team speculated. The mineral was indeed the cornerstone of their technological achievements, enabling their mastery of space travel and advanced energy systems.

Not only that. All the architecture, designs, and systems that were required to build the spaceships, starships and vessels originated from the mineral Quantium-42. The ancient civilisation catalogued everything that they built, so we, their ancestors could follow in their footsteps if needed. We have everything they knew.

"This material might have been their oil," Torsten said, gesturing to a projection of the civilisation's hypothetical energy grid. "It powered their progress, but it could also have contributed to their downfall. If their reliance on it accelerated their climate crisis, we need to learn from that. The question is how? How could this material have accelerated their climate crisis? How could a clean energy source have contributed to changing their climate, the,... biosphere? Could mining the material inadvertently disrupt and release gases deep within the Earth's crust?... No action, without a reaction."

Torsten was correct.

Mining Quantium-42 released gases. These include methane gas. Methane ($CH_4$) is a potent greenhouse gas, about eighty-four times more powerful than $CO_2$ when viewed over twenty years. It originates from natural sources and human activities. Due to its strong heat absorption, even short-lived methane significantly impacts the biosphere.

As the team of *Deep Explorer* prepared for its next mission, they knew they had only scratched the surface of Quantium-42's potential. They are also starting to realise massive quantities of methane are released when extracting Quantium-42. The journey ahead would test not only their scientific ingenuity but also their ethical resolve. The energy revolution had begun, and the world would never be the same.

Would history repeat itself, as it had for the ancient civilisation?

# 7

# Cycles

G EORGE had uncovered something unexpected, deep within the repository of knowledge, encoded in junk DNA.

The screen was flashing red!

Then an audible alert beeped, getting louder and louder.

An incoming celestial event that demanded immediate attention was discovered.

Dr Torsten Berg leaned forward, his hands gripping the edge of the console as the computer systems deciphered projections filled the main screen. A comet, named Icarus-Theta-2, was charting a trajectory that would bring it extremely close to Earth's orbit. Extremely close in astronomical terms.

The system had run additional models itself, after discovering the knowledge from the ancient civilisation, deep in the junk DNA.

As the comet passes through the asteroid belt between Earth and Mars, its gravitational pull could disrupt several large asteroids, one of which was on a 98% probability collision course with Earth.

How could the ancient civilisation have known this?

The room erupted in a flurry of anxious voices. While Earth had faced asteroid threats before, the data accompanying this prediction was particularly alarming.

The projected impact date is fifty years from now. The asteroid's size, combined with its velocity, would result in devastation on a planetary scale.

"It's eerily similar," Torsten said grimly, referencing the catastrophe that had wiped out the ancient civilisation they'd been uncovering. "A climate and biosphere crisis compounded by an asteroid strike. It's like history is repeating itself. If we mine and drill the mineral Quantium-42, that will release more and more methane, leading to Earth's demise, again. But without mining Quantium-42, we'll never be able to produce the required amount of energy to save ourselves, leave the planet. To survive as a species we have to leave Planet Earth. To leave the planet we must mine and use Quantium-42. But mining Quantium-42 will destroy the biosphere on Earth. But the Earth will be destroyed by the asteroid impact anyway. It's almost as if Earth, Mother Nature herself, is nudging us to leave, why?"

Dr. Elise DuPont nodded, her face pale. "We're just as unprepared for this as they were."

The team began discussing possible responses. Deflection missions, planetary defence systems, and international cooperation. But the realisation dawned on everyone. Even with modern technology, humanity's ability to prevent such a catastrophe was limited. Time was running out, and so was the margin for error. The screen flashed red, showing the 98% probability of the asteroid and comet trajectories.

A sombre mood settled over the team. As they worked, conversations turned from technical problem-solving to broader reflections on humanity's place.

Why is history repeating?

How can history repeat itself?

Is this fate?

Were we always meant to find this knowledge now?

Elise stood in the observation room later that night, staring at the stars above the dark ocean. Torsten joined her. "Do you think this is fate?" she whispered. Her voice was barely audible.

Torsten hesitated before responding. "I think it's cycles. Nature doesn't play favourites. Civilisations rise and fall, and the universe just keeps moving. But, I'm starting to think there's something else going on, call it fate, or destiny. There's something, something I just don't think we'll ever be able to know or explain."

The discovery of the ancient civilisation, coupled with the looming asteroid threat, forced the team to confront uncomfortable truths.

Was humanity doomed to repeat the same mistakes as its predecessors?

Could they break free from the cyclical nature of history? Maybe it was fate for Earth to go through these cycles.

Are civilisations inherently doomed to self-destruction?

The ancient civilisation had been advanced enough to harness interstellar travel, yet they were ultimately undone by a combination of environmental collapse and cosmic misfortune.

As the days passed, the team began to see the clear parallels between their own situation and that of the ancient civilisation. Both had faced existential threats, both had possessed the technological means to respond, and both had been caught off guard by the scale of the challenge. To save themselves, they will have to be partly responsible for destroying Earth's biosphere and climate.

Elise gathered the team. "The ancients left us their knowledge so we would learn and have the information needed to survive. They knew history would repeat itself, at some time. That time is now. In fifty years, there's a 98% probability the Earth will be uninhabitable for humans, because of the asteroid strike. Their knowledge will save us." she said. "They wanted us to learn, to be better. But knowledge without action is meaningless. We have the tools, but do we have the will? But, and this is a but, there is also a 2% chance the asteroid doesn't materialise, let me repeat, doesn't materialise and make Earth uninhabitable. If that's the case, we alone would have destroyed the biosphere by mining Quantium-42. But destroying Earth would have been for nothing if, and it's a big if, the asteroid doesn't impact. Maybe we should be focused on deflecting or destroying the asteroid."

Dr Torsten interrupted. "Elise, if we destroy the asteroid the resulting debris has an almost 100%, in fact 99.98% probability of hitting Earth. Who knows how big those chunks will be? Everyone in the room was silent. "And, the only way to generate enough energy to deflect the asteroid would be to use Quantium-42. And we all know, to mine Quantium-42 in enough quantities will destroy the biosphere. Destroyed for at least ten million years, until Earth rejuvenates".

Their words sparked a renewed sense of purpose among the crew. The comet and asteroid weren't just threats, they were tests. Humanity's response would determine whether it was destined to follow the same path as the ancients or whether it could forge a new trajectory.

# 8

# Knowledge

The control room of the *Deep Explorer Lab Rig* had transformed into a war room of ideas. Equipment chimed and buzzed. Control systems flickered and glinted.

On one side of the debate were those who believed the discovery of the fossilised microchip and Quantium-42 needed to be disclosed to the world immediately. On the other side were those who feared the chaos such revelations might unleash.

Around the room, holographic displays projected simulations, data charts, and theoretical models, an overwhelming flood of information underscoring the gravity of their decisions.

Dr Elise DuPont stood, weary-faced, at the centre of the room. "Let's establish what we know," she said, projecting a list onto the central screen.

The Microchip. Evidence of an advanced civilisation that predated humanity by 500 million years.

Encoded DNA. A direct connection between that civilisation and modern humans.

Quantium-42. A revolutionary energy source with the potential to transform, or destabilise the world. But, climate-destroying methane is released when mining it.

"This isn't just a scientific discovery," Elise continued. "It's a global paradigm shift. We need to decide if, and how, this knowledge is shared."

Torsten Berg argued passionately for disclosure. "The truth belongs to everyone," he said. "This discovery could unify humanity, give us a shared origin story, and push us toward collaboration instead of division."

"But what if it does the opposite?" countered Dr. Martin Knight, the environmental economist. "Think about the geopolitical implications of Quantium-42 alone. Entire economies are built on oil, coal, and gas. If we disrupt that overnight, the fallout could be catastrophic wars, economic collapses, mass unemployment."

The room grew tense as the conversation turned to the potential societal consequences of revealing the microchip and Quantium-42.

Dr Knight outlined how the sudden introduction of Quantium-42 could destabilise industries and nations reliant on fossil fuels. "The countries that control this new material will hold unprecedented power. Do we trust them to wield it responsibly?"

Several team members worried that governments or corporations might monopolise Quantium-42, leading to inequality and new forms of exploitation.

Some feared that access to Quantium-42-powered technologies could widen the gap between wealthy and impoverished nations, further entrenching global inequalities.

But what would that matter if the Earth is to be destroyed in fifty years?

Dr. Mary Lopez, an anthropologist, raised another dimension of the debate. "If we disclose the microchip and its connection to human DNA, we're challenging deeply held beliefs about creation, purpose, and the uniqueness of humanity."

She continued, "Religions around the world teach that humanity is special, often divinely created. How will people react when they learn we're the product, or partially the product of an ancient civilisation's genetic engineering? It could be enlightening, or deeply destabilising. If the ancient civilisation were also humans, the same as we are, the implications are profound."

Others argued that such a revelation could inspire humanity to see itself as part of a greater cosmic story. "This could bring people together," Torsten suggested. "If we understand that we're all connected, not just to each other but to an ancient civilisation, it might foster a sense of shared responsibility."

A smaller but vocal group advocated for keeping the discoveries classified. Dr. Alexis Tan, a security specialist, warned of the dangers of making such powerful knowledge public.

"Imagine if a rogue nation or terrorist group got their hands on Quantium-42," Alexis said. "It could be weaponised in ways we can't even imagine. The risks are astronomical."

She concluded, "Sometimes, knowledge is too dangerous to share. We can study this material in secret, develop safeguards, and release it when humanity is ready if that day ever comes.

For the first time, Elise disclosed she's had to inform people higher up in the chain of command. Way, way up in the chain. With no ifs or buts, she's been told everything happening on the Deep Explorer is of utmost national importance. National Security.

Everyone onboard has been given a temporary clearance of Top Secret, but only for discussions, data and discoveries on board. No access to other material or projects. The team's reminded of any leaks of any kind, and they're likely to end up in a black site or Gitmo 2.0.

If it was serious enough already, it just got a hell of a lot more serious.

Elise further explained what the higher-ups told her. "So, the plan is first, that Quantium-42's discovery would be disclosed selectively. Focusing on its energy potential while withholding its connection to the ancient civilisation. And second, the microchip and its link to human DNA would remain classified, Top Secret, until further studies were completed and a strategy for responsible disclosure was developed."

Elise summarised their decision. "We're not hiding the truth," she said. "We're managing it. The world isn't ready for the full story, but that doesn't mean it won't be, someday."

Elise lingered in the observation room, staring out at the dark ocean. Torsten joined her, silent at first, before finally speaking.

"Do you think we made the right choice?" he asked.

"I don't know," Elise admitted. "I just don't know."

Far away, the government teams from the Five Eyes intelligence alliance listened and watched. "She's done the right thing," said one of the agents. "Let's keep an eye on her and her team. We have to trust that they'll do the right thing. We can't let them know, that we know everything they know. They've done the leg work for us".

# 9

# Fermi and Gaia

The monumental discoveries of the Quantium-42, the fossilised microchip, and the encoded knowledge stored in our human DNA had opened up a Pandora's box.

It was inevitable that the discussions would eventually circle back to the Fermi Paradox and the Gaia Hypothesis, two profound concepts that seemed more relevant now than ever before.

Through arm-twisting consensus, it was decided only to disclose the discovery of Quantium-42 to the general public.

The fossilised microchip was kept secret from public disclosure. This in turn included the knowledge that junk DNA contains all the known knowledge from the advanced civilisation. This was deemed to be Above Top Secret knowledge, even though 20 people associated with *Deep Explorer* were known to have knowledge of this finding. The risks to humanity, and society were too great to disclose anything other than Quantium-42.

Dr. Torsten Berg initiated the discussion during an evening briefing. His holographic display shows a detailed star map of the Milky Way. "The Fermi Paradox asks a deceptively simple question," he began. "If the universe is so vast, and intelligent life so probable, then where is everyone?"

The team had no shortage of opinions. The discoveries from the Mariana Trench provided a fresh perspective on the paradox.

Elise DuPont posited that intelligent civilisations, like the one evidenced by the microchip, might rise and fall in cycles. "Perhaps civilisations are far more fragile than we assume," she said. "Environmental collapse, resource depletion, or cosmic events like asteroid impacts could limit their longevity. This seems to be the conundrum with Quantium-42, mining and drilling for this clean energy source inadvertently releases massive amounts of planet-changing methane. It's ironic."

Others argued that advanced civilisations might inevitably destroy themselves. Dr Martin Knight pointed to the climate crisis described in the ancient civilisation's encoded data. "If they couldn't avoid it, with all their advancements, what hope do we have?"

Alexis Tan introduced another possibility. "What if civilisations deliberately isolate themselves? Maybe they see the risks of interstellar communication as outweighing the benefits. It's possible the silence of the cosmos is intentional."

Torsten gestured to the microchip's engravings. "Or maybe," he added, "they leave behind relics or messages. A kind of cosmic breadcrumb trail for those who come after them. Due to time and distance, intelligent life and otherworldly civilisations are destined never to meet, giving the impression there is no one else, I mean, when we look at a planet orbiting a star ten million light-years away, the light that reaches us reveals what was happening there 10 million years ago. Since that time, ten million years have passed on that planet, and its current state remains unknown to us. Even if intelligent life and civilization have emerged there recently, any knowledge of their existence would take ten million years to reach us. Our understanding is perpetually locked in that planet's distant past. And according to GEORGE, we don't have ten million years! We've got fifty years to leave the Earth. Fifty!"

The team was left pondering a chilling thought.

What if the ancient civilisation was humanity's only predecessor in the galaxy, the universe?

What if the silence wasn't evidence of absence, but of singularity? The Earth is one of a kind.

The discussion shifted as Dr. Mary Lopez brought up the Gaia Hypothesis. First proposed by James Lovelock, which viewed Earth as a self-regulating system, where living organisms interact with their environment to maintain the conditions necessary for life. "The idea of Earth as a living entity," she said, "takes on a new dimension when we consider Quantium-42."

The team explored the implications of the Gaia Hypothesis in light of their discoveries.

Quantium-42's formation deep within the Earth suggested a process that required immense pressure and specific conditions over millions and millions of years. "It's as if Earth itself created Quantium-42 as part of its natural processes," Mary speculated. "Could it be that Earth produces such materials to support life's continuation? But in order to use the life-saving mineral, planet-destroying gases are released, to enable the Earth to start over, start from scratch. A clean slate. At the point a civilisation finds and uses Quantium-42, it's Mother Nature's way of pressing the reset button. I trip wire for a reset."

Elise pointed to the ancient civilisation's exodus and the eventual rejuvenation of Earth. "Gaia theory would suggest that Earth, left to its own devices, has the ability to recover. The fossil record supports this, life always finds a way to bounce back after mass extinctions."

The encoded DNA served as a stark reminder that while Earth might endure, civilisations may not. "We are stewards of this planet," Mary said, "but we're also incredibly vulnerable. Gaia can survive without us, but we cannot survive without Gaia."

As the team delved deeper into the connections between the Fermi Paradox and Gaia Theory, a profound realisation began to take shape.

Is Earth a rare haven?

The unique combination of conditions that allowed Quantium-42 to form, and life to thrive, suggested that Earth might be exceptionally rare, or the only one in the galaxy, in the universe.

If humanity was part of a long chain of technologically advanced civilisations, then its responsibility was not just to preserve life from Earth but to prepare for the next stage of its evolution, whether on Earth or beyond it.

Is that the reason?

Humans have to seed life throughout the universe, from Earth. The rise and fall of civilisations, the cycles of extinction and renewal, and the self-regulating nature of Earth seemed to reflect a universal rhythm.

Was this the way life always played out, everywhere in the cosmos?

If Earth isn't unique, and there are other Earth-like planets, is this what happens on those planets too?

Is Earth unique?

If life and intelligence were as fragile as the evidence suggested, perhaps Earth was not just rare but singular, a lone beacon in a vast and indifferent universe.

What is humanity's purpose?

Is humanity's purpose to simply survive and pass on genetic code?

Was humanity destined to follow the same path as its ancient predecessors, or could it break the cycle and create a sustainable future?

The encoded DNA hinted at a kind of immortality, not for individuals, but for civilisations. The ancients had ensured that their knowledge would survive, even if they did not.

Could modern-day humanity do the same?

# 10

# Frontiers

PRIVATE SPACE EXPLORATION COMPANY

The discovery of Quantium-42 sent ripples of excitement and anxiety through the scientific community.

The fossilised microchip and junk DNA knowledge store was secret. Above Top Secret.

The CEO of the private space exploration company was one of the twenty people who was entrusted with the secret knowledge.

The CEO started to use this knowledge to steer the company to design and manufacture systems and spacecraft, based on the ancient civilisations encoded DNA knowledge. The CEO was always seen as a genius, but even more now. Someone who could seemingly come up with miracles. He was a genius of sorts, but the source of his newfound genius was known to the remaining nineteen people. They knew the whole truth.

The focus shifted to practical implications. What the material could mean for the global economy and the future of science. As debates raged on how to introduce Quantium-42 to the world, two major fronts emerged. The economic impact of this revolutionary resource and the scientific breakthroughs it could enable.

Dr Martin Knight stood in front of a large projection displaying global energy markets. The display bristled with graphics that tingled and sparkled. The chart was divided into wedges representing oil, coal, natural gas, nuclear power, and renewables. He tapped a section of the display, and a glowing wedge labelled "Quantium-42" began to expand, rapidly overtaking the others.

"This is what the world could look like in fifty years if Quantium-42 becomes the primary energy source," he began. "But the transition will be anything but smooth. In fifty years, the quantity of methane released by mining Quantium-42 will render life on Earth uninhabitable. It will be the same as a dead, lifeless, toxic planet."

Quantium-42, with its limitless clean energy potential, promised to revolutionise the way humanity powered its world. But the implications for the global economy, climate and human civilisation were both absolutely staggering.

The fossil fuel industry, worth trillions of dollars, would likely collapse.

But would this matter, knowing the asteroid coming our way?

Should we keep the home fires burning, and pretend everything is ok?

Carry on as normal, give the illusion all is ok. Entire nations whose economies depended on oil and gas exports, such as Saudi Arabia, Russia, and Venezuela, would face economic upheaval.

Control of Quantium-42 deposits would dictate power in the new energy order. The Mariana Trench itself could become a contested site, as nations vie for access to its resources. It's likely major nations will start wars to enable access to the supply of Quantium-42 in The Mariana Trench.

Industries reliant on fossil fuels, automotive, aviation, and shipping would need to rapidly adapt or perish. Traditional renewable energy technologies might become obsolete overnight.

Again, does this matter given the incoming asteroid? Or, for window dressing, it does indeed matter to the world population, so the civilisation doesn't realise what is coming.

Methane release while mining for Quantium-42 is the one factor that will tip the balance for Earth. When mining for the miracle material, climate-changing and biosphere-destroying methane gas is released, in massive quantities. Quantities so large, that the methane can't be captured or used. In an ideal world, it would be. But the energy required to capture the methane, and materials to store it, is always more than available power, even using Quantium-42. It's a true conundrum.

The methane release is not focused in one area but over an impossibly large surface area of the sea bed. This massively complicates things. The gas is also released at over fifty kilometres below the Earth's crust, with the resulting pressure changes resulting in gas ejections that rise many tens of kilometres into the atmosphere. This is due to the resulting gas expansion bursting from fifty kilometres deep, through the eleven kilometres depth of the ocean and then bursting through the surface of the sea to the upper atmosphere. Bursting with the equivalent force and energy release of over 250 Hiroshima atomic bombs.

Computer models have predicted only 5% of released methane can be captured. That leaves 95% of all released methane when mining Quantium-42, entering the atmosphere and irreversibly changing the biosphere. Bursting like champagne at the F1 podiums with evil ferocity.

It's a cruel irony. The only solution to stop the methane release is to stop mining Quantium-42. But, not mining Quantium-42 means our species, the whole civilisation not be able to leave Earth. To survive the coming asteroid collision, Quantium42 needs to be mined. We must survive, we pass on our genetic code. That is our mission, our purpose.

What to do?

Dr. Knight posed the critical question: "How do we introduce Quantium-42 without destabilising the world economy? Do we phase it in gradually, or do we take the plunge and let everything fall where they may?"
The team discussed the ethics of economic control.

Should a global coalition oversee Quantium-42's distribution to prevent monopolisation?

Should corporate interests inevitably dominate, as they had with every major resource in history?

Quantium-42-powered generators could replace all fossil fuel plants, providing energy grids with unmatched efficiency. Portable Quantium-42 cells could revolutionise everything from consumer electronics to disaster relief efforts, enabling energy independence in remote or impoverished regions. Space propulsion systems utilising Quantium-42's quantum disruption properties will enable travel to Mars and beyond in a fraction of the time currently required.

The encoded DNA left behind by the ancient civilisation offered a treasure trove of information about their technology, biology, and culture. Advances in sequencing technology would be necessary to unlock the full potential of this genetic library. Partnerships with institutions like the Francis Crick Institute and CERN were already being discussed. Collaborations with organisations like NASA and JPL were also proposed to study Quantum-42's applications in creating stable wormholes or manipulating gravitational fields. But, the cloak of secrecy by partnering with these institutions could cause irreparable damage. Five Eyes would never allow it.

As the discussions unfolded, the team recognised the delicate balance between progress and peril. Dr. Mary Lopez warned, "Every scientific revolution comes with unintended consequences. We've seen it with nuclear energy, with artificial intelligence. We can't afford to be reckless."

The encoded DNA and store of knowledge served as a reminder of what could go wrong. The ancient civilisation had harnessed incredible technologies but had ultimately succumbed to environmental collapse and cosmic catastrophe. The parallels to humanity's current trajectory were impossible to ignore.

Elise DuPont raised a crucial point during one of the final debates. "Do we treat Quantum-42 and the encoded DNA as global assets, belonging to all of humanity? Or do we allow nations and corporations to exploit them for their own gain?"

An international coalition could oversee Quantum-42's development, ensuring equitable distribution and funding of scientific research that benefited all.

Without regulation, competition for Quantum-42 could lead to resource wars, deepening global inequalities and driving the world toward instability.

Standing on the rooftop helicopter landing pad, looking over the cityscape, Elise and Torsten both stared out across the horizon. The humid air is thick and watery. Contrasting with the cool conditioned air they've been in all day.

# II

# Past Ghosts

The storm coming was due to be one of the strongest on record. The team knew they had to button things up, as evacuation orders were used.

The wind and rain had already caused havoc to the islands it had passed.

The sky was a kaleidoscope of colours, as usually happens before storms in this region.

The *Deep Explorer Drilling Ship* drifted silently above the Mariana Trench. The occasional creak and yawn from the steel and titanium hull. Within its hull, the team was engaged in reflective discussion. Technical jargon billowing through the cabins.

As more fragments of the encoded DNA were decrypted, the story of the ancient civilisation became clearer. Their rise, triumphs, and eventual collapse mirrored patterns that seemed eerily familiar to humanity's own projected history.

Dr Elise DuPont stood before a display projecting timelines of Earth's major civilisations. Sumerians, Egyptians, Greeks, Romans, and the industrialised nations of the modern era. Superimposed over these were extrapolated timelines of the ancient civilisation, reaching far back over 500 million years ago.

"What we're seeing here," Elise began, "is a cycle. Civilisations rise through innovation, expand through exploitation of resources, and collapse when those resources are depleted or when external forces intervene."

Dr. Torsten Berg added, "The encoded data shows that the ancient civilisation's trajectory wasn't so different from ours. They developed agriculture, urban centres, and complex governance systems. Their technological advances were driven by the same factors that drive ours. Necessity, competition, and survival."

The team brainstormed whether this cyclic pattern was universal.

As resources become scarce, civilisations face crises that often lead to either collapse or transformation. The ancient civilisation had faced environmental degradation from overpopulation and energy consumption, challenges eerily similar to modern humanity's. Unintended consequences of mining and drilling for a clean energy source, inadvertently releasing planet-lethal methane.

The asteroid that struck their planet was a stark reminder that civilisations are also at the mercy of external, uncontrollable events, as well as events that can be controlled.

Dr. Mary Lopez raised the question of whether these patterns were rooted in biological instincts. "Is the drive to expand and consume an inherent trait of intelligent life? If so, how do we break the cycle?"

The team turned its attention to the role of technology in shaping civilisations. From the knowledge and data within junk DNA, it was clear that the ancient civilisation's technological trajectory bore striking parallels to humanity's own.

The ancient civilisation's mastery of energy, genetics, and space travel had been driven by necessity. Climate challenges have forced them to innovate or perish, much like the pressures driving renewable energy and space exploration today.

Wars and conflicts have also accelerated technological advances. Torsten pointed out that many of humanity's greatest inventions, radar, the internet, and even nuclear power, had originated during periods of conflict. Necessity is the mother of invention.

The encoded history within the junk DNA revealed that the ancient civilisation had struggled with social inequalities, much like modern societies. Technological advancements often widened the gap between those with access to resources and those without.

This led to internal divisions that weakened their ability to respond to external threats, a cautionary tale for humanity.

Elise highlighted the paradox of progress. "Technology solves immediate problems but often creates new ones. The ancient civilisation harnessed incredible power with Quantium-42, but their reliance on it contributed to their ecological collapse, as the more they mined for it, the more methane gas was released ad infinitum."

Humanity's reliance on fossil fuels mirrored the ancient civilisation's reliance on their primary energy source. Quantium-42 offered hope, but massive risks also.

The interconnectedness of modern civilisation made it more vulnerable to systemic shocks, much like the centralised systems that had hastened the ancient civilisation's collapse.

Dr. Martin Knight summarised. "The ancient civilisation didn't fail because they were unintelligent or unprepared. They failed because they didn't recognise the limits of their own systems, and the unforeseen unintended consequences of mining Quantium-42, until it was too late. "

Torsten concluded, "The microchip and the DNA aren't just messages. They're warnings. The ancients are telling us that it's going to happen to us too. It's our fate. We can't escape our fate."

Standing on the observation deck, Elise and Torsten looked out over the endless ocean, their reflections illuminated by the stars.

"Do you think we can break the cycle, or is this fate?" Torsten asked.

# 12

# Legacy

The *Deep Explorer Surface Ship* floated in tranquil waters. Unusually still waters. The calm before the storm.

The moon shimmers off the smooth ocean surface. The stars above are brighter than they have been for a while, shining with bright intensity.

The team's mission is near completion.

Dr Elise DuPont addressed the team, her voice calm but resolute. "We've uncovered more than we ever imagined. The Quantium-42, the microchip, and encoded DNA. They're pieces of a puzzle, but they're also mirrors. They show us what we could be, and what we could lose."

Dr. Torsten Berg added, "They, the ancients, didn't just vanish. Their knowledge shaped us, even if we didn't realise it. And now, it's our responsibility to carry that legacy forward."

As the team looked to the future, they speculated on what their discoveries meant for Earth and humanity.

The Earth's self-regulating nature, as posited by the Gaia Hypothesis, suggested that the planet would endure, regardless of humanity's fate.

The encoded junk DNA showed that life, even after near-total extinction, could rise again.

The asteroid predicted to impact Earth in fifty years loomed large, like the Sword of Damocles.

Could humanity muster the global cooperation and technological ingenuity needed to avert catastrophe?

Quantium-42's energy potential offered hope for interstellar colonisation, mirroring the ancient civilisation's efforts to escape their doomed planet.

Was humanity destined to leave Earth, only to repeat the same cycle elsewhere?

The encoded DNA and the microchip raised the possibility that life on Earth, and perhaps throughout the cosmos, was seeded intentionally.

If humanity itself was the product of an ancient exodus, what did that mean for its identity?

Were humans truly Earthlings, or cosmic wanderers destined to perpetuate the cycle of life across the stars?

The team drafted their final report, emphasising the choices humanity now faced. Dr Martin Knight summarised their findings: "The ancients left us their story not to glorify their achievements, but to warn us. Progress without foresight is destruction. Unity without action is meaningless. We have the tools to survive, but only if we work together. We must survive."

The report urged global leaders to establish an international coalition to manage Quantium-42 responsibly. Invest in planetary defence systems to prepare for the threat of potential asteroid strikes.

Deep below, the *Deep Explorer Drilling Sub* and onboard team prepared to surface for the final time.

Above the trench, on the sea surface, the team gathered on the observation deck.

Above them, the stars shimmered, silent witnesses to the rise and fall of countless civilisations. Just as the ship was starting to rise and fall, the auto-stabilising buoyancy was nearly at breaking point with the ensuing storm.

Torsten gazed at the heavens and spoke softly. "Do you think they're still out there? The ones who left for the stars?"

Elise nodded slowly. "Maybe. But even if we never meet them, they're part of us. Their story is our story now."

The ocean stretched endlessly before them, a reflection of the infinite possibilities that lay ahead. The cycle of life and civilisation might be eternal, but for the first time, humanity had a chance to shape its outcome consciously.

The unusually still waters had started to swirl. The calm before the storm had ended. The swell rose and the waves building, crashing against the titanium and steel hull. Crashing and smashing like an orchestra percussion, with rhythmic precision.

On the instructions of Elise, GEORGE sifted through a nugget of data. The output succinctly indicated that from the junk DNA knowledge store, an exodus by the ancient civilisation occurred. An exodus from Earth 500 million years ago. How many of them left in the exodus, and how they left Earth was yet to be discovered.

The legacy of the ancient civilisation was secure. Their knowledge and wisdom are ready to save us.

Now, the future of modern-day humans is destined to repeat the cycle of civilisations, our fate sealed.

It was our time to prepare for an exodus.

An exodus of Earth.

History was repeating itself, just like the ancient civilisation had to do.

This time, an exodus must take place within the next fifty years.

# After Foreword

I came up with the initial idea of this story many years ago. It's only now I thought about turning that initial idea into a story. The technology and wherewithal now, is a fairly realistic proposition, however finding a microchip inside a rock is rather fanciful...

The intention of writing and publishing this book is to get the idea and story out of my head and onto paper, so there is something to work with. I'll then revisit the story and turn it into a screenplay to either make a short film, full-length feature film or TV series. How this is done is yet to be decided.

It could take the format of human actors, with a mix of CGI/VFX, or a pure animated film in the style of Akira. I've always liked the style of the animations from the 90s like Akira.

After that is done, I can see books two and three starting with the title "Deep" being written and also turned into screenplays. Book two will be called Deep Exodus. Book three will be called Deep Return.

I am very grateful to people that I admire who have inspired and helped me with writing. Also, the courage to just go for it. I also want physical things for my family, especially my son if and when I die. These people all know who they are, and many others, who don't know they helped me, but inspired me. Thank you.

# References

FURTHER READING

1. https://www.britannica.com/place/Mariana-Trench

2. https://www.bbc.co.uk/news/articles/c7vd1zjlr5lo

3. https://en.wikipedia.org/wiki/Alpha_Centauri

4. https://en.wikipedia.org/wiki/Proxima_Centauri_b

5. https://news.sky.com/story/the-wonder-material-which-could-hold-the-key-to-near-limitless-energy-13290834

# Sneak Peek (Book 2)

## Deep Exodus

*Fifty years after the discoveries in "Deep Fate," humanity faces extinction from an impending asteroid and environmental collapse caused by Quantium-42, a revolutionary material that both advanced and endangered civilisation. This material, once a beacon of technological progress, now drives Earth towards being uninhabitable due to toxic emissions from its extraction. With the planet's doom imminent humans have to exodus planet Earth.*

# Sneak Peek (Book 3)

## Deep Return

*Humanity arrives at its destination, uncovering remnants that reveal an ancient, cyclical mission. The mission is to regenerate life on Earth. This rebirth spans vast stretches of time and space. The vessel carries the essential building blocks of life, destined to reach a rejuvenated Earth and usher in a new era. Deep Return explores the majestic cycles of life and the universe, delving into the intertwining of time, space, history, and legacy.*

# The Author

William H. D. Coleman is a UK-based, author. He blends thrillers with hard science fiction, technology, military and espionage. His broad tapestry of international experiences, multilingual interactions, and diverse acquaintances infuse his stories.

# The Book

In the near future, an expedition deep in the Mariana Trench uncovers a groundbreaking mineral. This discovery prompts urgent questions and ethical decisions. As secrets that could reshape our understanding of history and the future come to light, **"Deep Fate"** offers a thought-provoking exploration of our past, legacy and future.

www.ingramcontent.com/pod-product-compliance
Ingram Content Group UK Ltd.
Pitfield, Milton Keynes, MK11 3LW, UK
UKHW041015120225
455007UK00004B/115